# I Am Papa Snap and These Are My Favorite No Such Stories

Delacorte Press

New York

# I AM PAPA SNAP

### and These Are My Favorite

# NO SUCH STORIES

**TOMI UNGERER**

Whipped Up, Drawn, and Dramatized by

# For YVONNE

Published by
Delacorte Press
Bantam Doubleday Dell Publishing Group, Inc.
666 Fifth Avenue
New York, New York 10103
Copyright © 1971 by Tomi Ungerer
Published by arrangement with Diogenes Verlag AG Zurich
All rights reserved. No part of this book may be reproduced or transmitted in any form
or by any means, electronic or mechanical, including photocopying, recording, or by any information storage
and retrieval system, without the written permission of the Publisher,
except where permitted by law.
The trademark Delacorte Press® is registered in the U.S. Patent and Trademark Office.

**Library of Congress Cataloging-in-Publication Data**
Ungerer, Tomi [date of birth]
I am Papa Snap and these are my favorite no such stories /
whipped up, drawn, and dramatized by Tomi Ungerer.
p.      cm.
Summary: In these nonsense episodes Papa Snap is eaten by a sofa,
Uncle Rimsky lights his cigars with dragons
and Mr. Tuber Sprout gets up to miss the train every morning.
ISBN 0-385-30653-9
[1. Humorous stories.] I. Title.
PZ7.U43Ib 1992      [E]—dc20      91-34658      CIP      AC

Typography by Lynn Braswell

Manufactured in the United States of America
June 1992
10  9  8  7  6  5  4  3  2  1
WOR

Bunny Bunson Brittle goes fishing.
He has no permit.
Who cares?
There are no fish.

**A**fter a violent argument with his parents
young Arson Twitch ran away from home,
taking along the family tub.
He set out to sea.
After three weeks and two days of nothing
he tried out his slingshot on a battleship.

**S**ir Spiffy Loin is famed for his
daring exploration of far-out jungles.
He hunts down wildflowers,
which he captures and tames.
On the western slopes of the Kilimanjaro
he finally discovered the rarest of them all,
the giant carnivorous *Pedophagia spinatus*.
After countless adventures
Sir Spiffy Loin managed to return with his prize.
At last, following years of relentless work,
he was able to train the plant
to perform various acts in public.

The four Tremblance brothers,
Fester, Fister, Faster, and Foster,
love to blast their helicons.
It sounds terrible.
All the tenants of the building
they live in had to move out.
They just could not stand
the hideous noise anymore.
"Great," says Fister, the oldest brother.
"Now we have the building to ourselves."

TREMBLANCE BROTHERS
PERFORM BEFORE
THE PRESIDENT

FUN, FAME AND
PROFIT AT THE
WHITE-HOUSE

Mr. and Mrs. Kaboodle went to town
to purchase a new nest. They bought one
for sale from a local nidologist.
It was a brand-new model which came with
plumbing and ready-laid eggs.
The Kaboodles had it promptly delivered to
the tree they owned upstate.
But
the nest fell apart in a week.
The eggs, which were rotten, started to leak.
The plumbing was useless since it
just consisted of a piece of pipe with a spigot.
"Well, that's what happens when
you start spending money,"
reflected Mr. Kaboodle sadly.

**M**r. Maroon Morsel gave his wife Retina a steamroller
for their twentieth anniversary.
She uses it to iron out her laundry
and flatten pizza dough.
They drive it on weekends to visit Mr. Morsel's
bedridden mother who lives in the mountains.

**W**hen Mr. Slop Gut visits his favorite restaurant
he orders everything on the menu.
The other night he put on so much weight during his meal
that he crashed through the floor on his way out.

Mr. Lido Rancid went to see his doctor,
Stigma Lohengreen. "Doctor," he lamented,
"I can't breathe. I feel clogged,
and my thorax is peppered with pains."
The medicine man took him into the X-ray machine,
and pondered over the patient's inside.
"There is a PICKLE jammed in your vena cava,
and the gangliated chords of your sympathetic
are all tangled up. Here is your prescription,"
said the doctor. "It is a pickle tune.
Sing it three times a day before meals. Good-bye."

The prescription did not work,
and Mr. Rancid got much worse.
By now he has already worn out
two beds and three nurses.

**M**r. Limpid is blind.
Mrs. Limpid is lame.
They are old.
They are happy.
They have each other.

Uncle Rimsky never believed in dragons
until he discovered one behind an abandoned tractor.
It was weak, limp, and shaky.
Uncle Rimsky took it into his home
and fed it with matches and kindling wood.
This ingenious diet soon restored the dragon.
The grateful beast now works very nicely
lighting Uncle Rimsky's cigars,
starting the fires in the morning,
and keeping the dishes hot.

Every morning Mr. Tuber Sprout runs to the station,
and every morning he misses the train.
In seven years he hasn't managed yet to get on the train.
"The station clock is always five minutes ahead of mine,"
he exclaims. "But at least it keeps me from going to work."

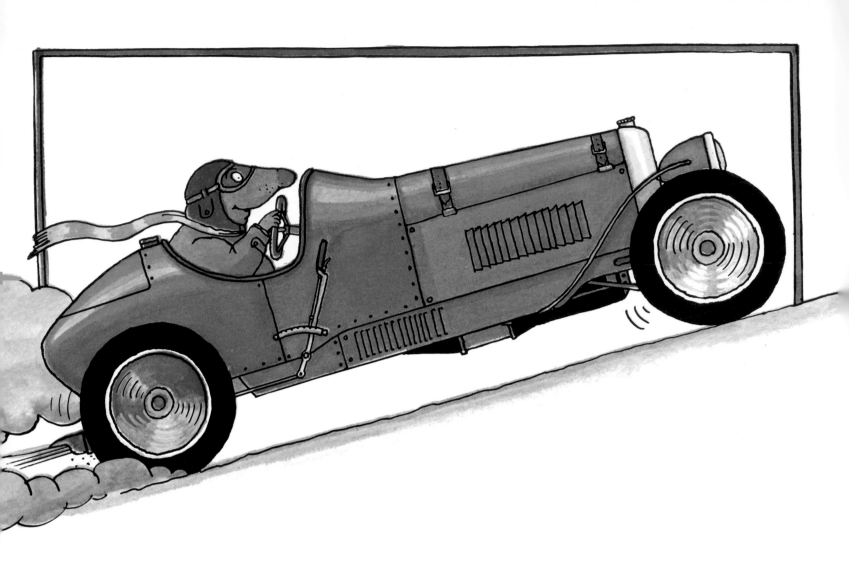

Zink Slugg bought a new car.
It had lots of cylinders,
coordinated cram-notch gears,
coupled crunch-brakes, two-speed grinders,
cobra upholstery,
an electronic police detector,
strobe headlights, and a quantity of whatnots.
It makes him feel very good.
But the day he rammed into a tree
it made him feel very bad.

After a bitter fight
Ace-Captain Vertigo's plane was hit.
He had already abandoned his
machine, when he realized
that he had left his
parachute at the canteen.
"I promise this is the last time
I'll forget my…"
SPLASH!

"Holy kayak," exclaimed Andy Rondak
as he returned from the supermarket
on a Wednesday afternoon
after a hard day's work at the ice cream factory
four miles down the road second turn to the left
after the pink gasoline station
which is now under new management
since nobody around here uses any gasoline
due to the fact that all the traffic is handled by
reindeers and dogs, a blessing too
when one considers how loud snowmobiles can be
which is one of the reasons why
the new management turned the gasoline station
into a library for the elderly.
"Holy kayak," exclaimed Andy Rondak.
"There is an elephant in my igloo."

Every day,
rain, shine, or overcast,
he walks down to the shore.
He sits on a rock to read or dream.
He has no friends, no enemies.
He lives in peace.
No one knows anything about him.
Not even his name.

One day Papa Snap heard of a very hungry sofa,
owned by a Mr. Mulch.
"What a wonderful No Such Story that would make!"
he thought.
That same night Papa Snap paid a visit to Mr. Mulch,
and was never seen again.